SPINNING OUT

ROAD
TRIP

SPINNING
OUT

R. T. MARTIN

DARBY CREEK
MINNEAPOLIS

Darby Creek
An imprint of Lerner Publishing Group, Inc.
241 First Avenue North
Minneapolis, MN 55401 USA

For reading levels and more information, look up this title at
www.lernerbooks.com.

Image credits: Master3D/Shutterstock.com, (winding road); Staras/Getty Images, (car); MihailUlianikov/Getty Images, (crystals); Dimitrina Lavchieva/Shutterstock.com, (climbers).

Main body text set in Janson Text LT Std 12/17.5.
Typeface provided by Adobe Systems.

Library of Congress Cataloging-in-Publication Data

Names: Martin, R. T., 1988– author.
Title: Spinning out / R.T. Martin.
Description: Minneapolis : Darby Creek, [2020] | Summary: Facing a severe snowstorm while on winter break in Colorado, friends CJ and Leo, Alex and Katrina, whose relationship is already in trouble, must rely on each other to survive.
Identifiers: LCCN 2018041017 (print) | LCCN 2018048273 (ebook) | ISBN 9781541557017 (eb pdf) | ISBN 9781541556850 (lb : alk. paper)
Subjects: | CYAC: Survival—Fiction. | Blizzards—Fiction. | Dating (Social customs)—Fiction. | Friendship—Fiction.
Classification: LCC PZ7.1.M37346 (ebook) | LCC PZ7.1.M37346 Ro 2019 (print) | DDC [Fic]—dc23

LC record available at https://lccn.loc.gov/2018041017

Manufactured in the United States of America
1-46119-43494-5/15/2019

For Meghan W.

CHAPTER 1

CJ heard a soft knock on her bedroom doorframe.

"Coffee?" Leo was holding two to-go cups from the coffee shop down the street.

"You're a lifesaver." She grabbed the cup he was holding out to her and took a sip. It was a vanilla latté, her favorite.

"You know, most of us pack the night *before* we go on a trip," Leo said, smiling. "Not the morning of."

"Shut up," CJ said through a giggle. "I was busy."

Leo's face scrunched up. "Busy with what? It's winter break."

She turned up her chin and took on a fake serious tone. "If you must know, there was an invasion that only I could stop."

Leo rolled his eyes. "Playing your new game again?" he asked. When she only grinned at him, he laughed. "Fair enough. You nearly done?"

CJ tossed a bottle of shampoo into her bag. "I am now!" she said and zipped the suitcase closed.

"May I?" Leo asked, gesturing toward the bag and bowing slightly.

"You may." CJ gave a slight curtsy.

Leo chuckled as he grabbed the bag. This was an inside joke that had been going on for nearly the entire two years they'd been dating. "When are Alex and Katrina getting here?" CJ asked as they went down the stairs.

"They're supposed to be here now," Leo replied. "I'd wonder what's keeping them, but . . ." He trailed off and gave CJ a knowing glance over his shoulder as they reached the bottom of the staircase.

She rolled her eyes. "I hope it's not that again."

"Hope it's not what again?" CJ's mom poked her head out from the kitchen.

"Nothing," CJ said quickly. "Alex and Katrina have just been having some . . . problems recently."

"Ah," her mom said. "Well, at least the trip should be fun. You all packed?"

"Yup!"

Leo put CJ's suitcase next to his by the front door. The one thing that CJ *had* done the night before was get her snowboard out. Now Leo's was next to it, all ready to go.

"You may want to call them and see where they are." CJ's dad was in the living room watching the morning news. "Looks like there's a storm that's set to hit pretty soon. You're going to want to get on the road sooner rather than later."

"Cool!" Leo said, excited. "Fresh powder!"

"Could make driving difficult," CJ's dad continued. "Judging by the forecast, it could be pretty bad."

Leo smiled and shook his head. "This station says every storm is going to be a disaster. How many times do they predict a blizzard, and all we get is an inch or two—sometimes nothing at all? I think they deliberately make the storms sound worse than they're going to be just to get more viewers and boost ratings."

"Still," CJ's dad said. "Better safe than sorry."

"You've got all the clothes you need?" her mom asked.

"Yes, Mom," CJ said, knowing it wouldn't be the last question. Her mom always went through a checklist every time CJ went out of town, even if they were going somewhere together.

"All the gear for your board?"

"Yup."

"Cell phone charger?"

"Yes, Mom, I've got everything I need." Out of the corner of her eye, she saw Leo take a sip of his coffee to conceal a smile. She gave him a little slap on the arm.

"Okay," her mom said. "Just wanted to

make sure." She paused. "You know how to get there? Do you want me to write down the address of the cabin just in case?"

"We're *fine*, Mom. We all have the address saved in our phones from when we went last year. And it's not hard to find, anyway. I'm sure Katrina knows how to get there, since it's her uncle's cabin."

Leo's phone buzzed. He pulled it out, looked at it, then spun around to look out the window. "They're here," he said.

"Have a good time, sweetie." Her mom pulled CJ in for a hug and a kiss on the forehead.

Her dad popped up from the couch and did the same. "You kids have fun. Don't do anything I wouldn't do."

"Oh," Leo said with a smile. "Did you start snowboarding recently?" He had been around so much for the past couple years that by now he easily fit in with CJ's whole family.

Her dad chuckled. "Okay, except that. You can do that." He gave Leo a friendly slap on the back as they gathered their suitcases and snowboards and headed outside.

Alex's blue minivan was parked in CJ's driveway, the engine still running, and CJ could see Katrina in the passenger seat. Right away, something seemed off. Katrina wasn't smiling. In fact, she looked like she was grinding her teeth in anger, but CJ hoped she was just imagining that.

Alex popped the trunk, and CJ and Leo loaded their bags on top of Alex and Katrina's suitcases and ski gear. When CJ came around the side of the car, Katrina had gotten out.

"I'm going to sit in the back with CJ," she said firmly.

"Do whatever you want," Alex said back to her. His cold tone told CJ everything she needed to know. The couple had been fighting.

CJ grimaced at Leo, but he just shrugged. He was always trying to downplay their friends' arguments. He probably figured everything would be fine once the trip got underway. CJ didn't feel as sure about that.

She hopped into the back seat behind Alex, and Katrina got in next to her, behind Leo.

"Colorado, here we come!" Leo said excitedly as Alex pulled out of the driveway. "Six hours from now, we'll be sliding down a mountain faster than a go-kart on steroids!" For a second, CJ thought he had just had too much coffee, but then she realized that he was probably trying to boost the mood in the car.

"That doesn't make any sense," Alex said flatly.

"It doesn't have to," Leo replied. "It's *extreme!*" He did something close to jazz hands. CJ giggled, but Alex just kept driving. Katrina didn't appear to be listening at all. She was staring out the window, but CJ could tell she wasn't really looking at anything in particular.

"Come on, you two," Leo continued. "It's winter break. We're about to spend the next four days hitting the slopes, and we don't have to worry about school for another week. This trip is going to be great."

Alex didn't respond, but Katrina turned toward the front seat, and CJ saw her roll her eyes.

CJ looked out her own window. Flurries had begun to fall from the gray sky. This was going to be a long trip.

CHAPTER
2

"Is it a fictional character?" CJ asked.

"No," Leo replied. Two and a half hours into the drive, the friends had already gone through two playlists and resorted to playing Twenty Questions.

"Is it a living thing?" Alex asked. It was the first time he'd actually spoken since Leo suggested playing the game. The previous two rounds had just been CJ asking all the questions while Alex watched the road and Katrina stared out her window.

"Uh, no," Leo said, caught off guard by Alex's question. Alex shrugged and kept his gaze on the road.

CJ, eager to keep going if Alex's mood was suddenly turning around, continued: "Is it a disease?"

Leo tilted his head suspiciously. "Yes . . ."

"Smallpox!" Alex shouted.

"Nope," Leo said, smiling.

"You didn't think you should narrow it down a little more first?" Katrina piped up.

Alex scowled a little. "If you want to sit back there and just criti—"

"Fifteen questions left," Leo practically shouted over Alex. "Use them wisely."

"Is there a cure?" CJ asked. She wanted to keep the game moving forward and not give Alex and Katrina a chance to start fighting again.

"No, I don't think so," said Leo. "Fourteen questions left."

"Does it only affect people?" Katrina asked.

Leo turned around to face her. "No."

"Is the other species it affects apes?" Katrina said immediately.

"Yes!" Leo replied.

"Ebola," Katrina said flatly. She returned to

staring out the window at the falling snow.

"Wow," CJ said. "How did you figure it out so quickly?"

"Remember during sophomore year when we had to do those presentations about infectious diseases?" CJ nodded. "Leo did Ebola. He also did the Spanish Inquisition for a presentation in history junior year. And Edgar Allen Poe, that was the author you wrote the essay about in Ms. Moen's English class, right?"

Leo smiled back at her. "I think she's on to me." CJ and Alex chuckled. Even Katrina cracked a smile.

"I've got an advantage in this game," Katrina said. "Leo and I have had a lot of classes together."

"And you've got a really good memory," Alex added.

CJ and Leo looked at each other. CJ was pleased to hear Alex compliment Katrina after they'd seemed so close to arguing this whole time. Leo shot her a look that roughly translated to *See—I told you everything would be fine.*

"Thanks," Katrina said to her boyfriend.

"How's the driving, Alex?" CJ asked.

The snow was falling steadily, building up on the road, but the lanes of traffic on the highway were still easily visible. Sometimes the wind would whip up and blow snow all over the place, making it difficult to tell where one lane ended and another began, but when it died down, everything became relatively clear again.

"It's okay," Alex said. "Nothing I can't handle."

"If you need someone to take over, just let me know," she offered.

He shrugged. "It looks worse than it is. I think I'll be able to handle the whole trip."

"Well, if you all think you can outsmart me again, I've come up with another answer for Twenty Questions," Leo said. He turned to face Katrina. "And this time, it's not something I did a project about. No more advantage for you. Think you can handle it?"

"Can you handle losing for the fourth time in a row?" Katrina asked with a smile.

Things seemed normal again. CJ was able to relax a little bit. In a few hours, they'd reach the cabin on Split Peak Mountain. They'd drop their bags off, drive a little farther to the Silver Springs ski resort, and hit the slopes. They could forget about their problems for the next four days . . . at least CJ hoped they could.

Things between Alex and Katrina had been pretty rough recently. Nearly all their arguments had to do with college. CJ and Leo happened to be interested in the same university, so it had been an easy enough decision for them to both apply and see what happened. Things weren't as simple for the other couple.

Katrina had her heart set on NYU, but Alex wanted to go to UCLA. For the past few months, Katrina had tried to convince Alex to go to New York with her, and Alex had tried to get her to come to Los Angeles. No matter what reasons one gave, the other wouldn't budge. They'd both ended up applying to both schools just to see what happened. But CJ knew that Katrina had never expected to get into

UCLA, and she'd heard from Leo that Alex had had the same thoughts about NYU.

This past month, though, Alex and Katrina had found out they'd both received early acceptances to both schools. If it hadn't caused them to bicker nearly every day since, CJ might have found the situation funny. Plus, she was having a hard time feeling *too* sorry for them when she was still waiting to hear from any of the colleges she had applied to.

CJ looked out her window at the snow falling and wondered if this peace would last. All she wanted from the weekend was to have some fun snowboarding with her friends—one last hurrah before they had to start buckling down for their last semester of school and getting ready for the future. She didn't think that was too much to ask.

"Chicken nuggets," Alex said, bringing CJ's attention back to the game. She had no idea what kinds of questions they'd been asking to get to an answer like *that*.

"Nope," Leo replied.

"Chicken tenders," Katrina said.

"Correct!"

"That's the same thing!" Alex protested.

"It is not the same thing," Leo said. "Chicken nuggets are small, and the chicken is ground up. Chicken tenders are long strips of whole chicken."

Alex shook his head and rolled his eyes, although CJ could tell he was smiling. "They're basically the same thing."

"But you acknowledge that they're not *exactly* the same thing," Leo replied. "And if Twenty Questions doesn't demand pinpoint accuracy, then what are we all doing here?"

"Sometimes I worry about you," Alex said.

"You should try dating him," CJ said.

Alex chuckled. "I'd rather not."

The wind picked up, and CJ felt the van swerve a little. Her stomach rose and dropped. She saw Alex grip the wheel tightly.

"Whoa," he said, correcting the vehicle's path. "That wind's getting nasty."

"Slow down if you need to," CJ said. "Better to get there late and safe than to never get there at all." Leo cocked an eyebrow at her, and CJ laughed at herself. "I can't believe I just said that. I'm becoming my dad." She saw Leo covering his laughter in the front seat.

"Okay, I've got one!" Alex said suddenly, bringing them back to their game. He sat up in his seat and wiggled his eyebrows at them through the rearview mirror. "You guys are never gonna guess this . . ."

* * *

A half hour later, Alex announced he had to stop for gas. He pulled off the highway and into a gas station. While he refilled the tank, the others headed inside to look for some snacks.

"Huh," Leo said, picking up a bag of beef jerky. "This comes in party lime flavor now." He paused. "What's the difference between party limes and regular limes?"

CJ looked up from the candy aisle. "Party limes wear hats."

"Sold!" Leo said with a grin.

They walked toward the checkout counter where Katrina was now joined by Alex. They were talking quietly, and CJ noticed they both looked frustrated.

"I don't want to talk about this anymore," Katrina said, her arms folded.

"Well, I do," Alex replied.

"This isn't the time or the place and you know it. The whole point of this trip was to take a break and relax for once. We can talk again after we get home."

Alex scoffed and opened his mouth to say something else. Judging by the look on his face, CJ knew he was going to keep pressing the issue.

She stepped forward and put on a fake smile. "Everything okay?" she asked, though she already knew the answer.

"It's fine," Katrina said forcefully and marched outside without buying anything.

Alex lingered around the counter until CJ and Leo were done buying their snacks. When they got outside, Katrina was leaned up against the van scrolling through her phone. CJ watched as Alex tried to catch Katrina's eye, but she kept her gaze on her phone. He rolled his eyes and stomped over to the driver's side door.

"Ready to go?" CJ asked her friend, hoping that some time with another person would put Katrina in a better mood.

Katrina's gaze slid sideways, toward Alex, but he was no longer watching her. She gave CJ a weak smile. "Yeah. Sorry about all this. I know you guys have been looking forward to this getaway as much as we have."

CJ looped her arm through Katrina's. "I just want you two to enjoy yourselves."

Katrina wrinkled her nose. "I'm a senior in high school who can't decide whether to go to my dream college thousands of miles away from my boyfriend or go to a college I don't like just because my boyfriend wants to go there. I don't think I remember the meaning of fun."

"Okay, drama queen," CJ said with a snort. She walked them over to the sliding doors of the van. "Let's get going and I'll try to remind you just how much fun you can be."

Alex was tense when they climbed in, but his shoulders loosened up as he noticed Katrina was laughing with CJ. Leo leaned over the back of his seat as the girls buckled in.

"I propose a new game," he said. "Would You Rather." Leo and CJ started bouncing questions off of each other, and after a couple rounds Katrina started quietly responding as well. Soon the three of them were cracking up over the most ridiculous questions they could come up with. Even Alex joined in laughing.

Katrina turned to CJ. "Would you rather be rejected from every college you've applied to or be accepted to your dream school but have Ms. Moen as your professor for every class?"

CJ chewed the side of her lip at that question. She didn't want to talk about college—not when it was still so uncertain for her and when it was causing so much conflict between Katrina and Alex. CJ tried to keep things as casual as she could. "I'll take the rejection," she said, forcing a smile. "One class and one year of Ms. Moen was more than enough."

"Agreed," Leo said.

Katrina giggled. "I guess that one was kind of easy."

"Your turn, CJ," Leo said.

"Alex," CJ started. "Would you rather lose all your books or never be able to use the internet again?" This wasn't exactly a difficult question, she knew, but she was just desperate to come up with something quickly. Anything to move the topic of conversation away from college and future plans.

"Please," Alex said. "I'll keep my books and lose the internet any day."

Katrina snorted. "You're, like, the only person I know who would choose books over the internet. Give me the internet any day!"

"Or you can try talking to people in the real world instead of following their posts and pictures on social media," said Alex.

"You know what I mean," Katrina snapped. "God, you make me sound so shallow."

Leo turned around to give CJ a look—they both knew they had to act quickly before this turned into another argument. "Hey, guys,"

CJ said. "How about another question? Alex, I think it's your turn."

"All right, I've got a question," he said. Judging by the tone of his voice, CJ had a feeling she wasn't going to like what he had to ask. "Katrina, would you rather go to New York by yourself or go to college with the guy you've been dating for three years?"

"Real mature, Alex," Katrina spat at him.

"Answer the question," Alex said, shrugging.

"Honestly, you're making New York look really appealing right now." CJ could see Katrina's face flushing.

"So, you're fine going four years without seeing each other? That's what you want to do?"

"Whose turn is it?" Leo said, trying to change the subject.

"Don't be so dramatic!" Katrina snapped at Alex. "We'd still see each other on breaks and during the summer. And we could see each other all the time if you just agreed to go to NYU!"

"Why should I have to agree to go to NYU if you won't agree to go to UCLA?" Alex turned back in the driver's seat to look at Katrina.

"Watch the road," CJ said, but Alex didn't seem to hear.

"I could ask you the same question," Katrina said, leaning forward as if she were trying to get into Alex's face.

"Twenty Questions was more fun." CJ couldn't tell if Leo was joking or if it was a legitimate attempt to break up the argument. "I've got one. You've got—"

"I'll bet if Adam Weis were going to UCLA, you'd go." Alex was still glaring into the back seat while driving.

"Watch the road!" CJ said a little louder.

"Oh my god," Katrina hissed. "We went to one movie together *freshman year*. Let it go! I don't even know where Adam is planning to go, and besides, that has nothing to do with this! You don't even know why you're mad!"

"I know why I'm mad!" Alex said. "I'm mad because you refuse to even think about—"

"Alex, watch the—" CJ wasn't able to finish before the van slid and began fishtailing.

Alex snapped forward and gripped the wheel. The van faced one way, then the other, while Alex desperately tried to correct its path. A car on their left honked and swerved to avoid slamming into the back of the van, which was halfway in the other lane. They swerved the other direction and for a moment, CJ thought they might spin all the way around and end up facing the wrong way in traffic.

The van slowed dramatically, and the car behind them had to quickly slide into the left lane to avoid rear-ending them. CJ heard the honk of the second car as it drove by.

Once the van was under control, Alex pulled over onto the shoulder. CJ realized her fists were clenched around the armrests. She was squeezing them harder than she'd thought she was capable of. The moment the van stopped moving, they all exhaled in relief.

"Everybody okay?" Leo asked.

"Yeah, I'm okay," Katrina answered.

"Me too," CJ said.

"I'm good," Alex said, although over his shoulder, CJ could see he was still gripping the steering wheel like his life depended on it.

"You nearly killed us!" Katrina shouted.

"Well, if you hadn't been yelling in my ear, I wouldn't have—"

"Enough!" CJ cut Alex off. "You're both to blame for what just happened. You started the argument, Alex, and then you nearly drove us off the road because you were arguing. And I don't know if you know this," she turned to Katrina, "but it takes *two* people to argue!"

Katrina looked down and started wringing her hands together. Alex went silent in the front seat.

CJ took a deep breath. "Look, I don't mean to yell, but the whole point of this trip was to *avoid* talking about stressful stuff like college decisions. None of us are going to have a good time unless you two remember how to get along."

"Maybe we should just call it off," Katrina said quietly.

"We're already over halfway there," Leo said. But he sounded disappointed, like he might have preferred turning back.

"Also, we already paid for the lift tickets, and they don't do refunds unless you give forty-eight hours' notice," CJ added. "Besides, you two *should* be able to get along. I feel like you've kind of lost sight of why you're fighting in the first place. It's *because* you care about each other and want to spend as much time together as possible. Which is sweet, but it's not exactly bringing out the best in you. I know it's hard to think about anything else. But please don't take out your frustrations on each other and on us right now. Please don't ruin this trip."

Both Alex and Katrina looked a little ashamed, and for a moment, CJ felt bad for scolding her friends, but she shook the feeling off. Their bickering had gotten out of hand, and someone had to say something.

Suddenly, there was a rapping against the driver's side window. Everyone jumped.

CJ's head whipped toward the window. A police officer was standing outside and motioning for Alex to roll the window down. He did, and bitter cold wind blasted into the car. CJ shivered in her seat.

"Everything all right here?" the officer asked. She peered through the window to look at everyone in the van. CJ held her breath, wondering if the officer had seen the spinout and suspected Alex of reckless driving. "Having car trouble?"

"No, Officer," Leo said. "We hit an icy patch of road and pulled over to collect ourselves for a second."

The officer nodded. "Where are you all heading?"

"A cabin on Split Peak Mountain," CJ said.

The officer frowned. "Wouldn't go that far if I were you. The storm's going to get a lot worse. Is there somewhere else you can stay? Somewhere closer?"

"Not really." Alex shrugged.

The officer looked down the road in the direction they were headed. "You already spun out once. In an hour or two, you might not be lucky enough to make it onto the shoulder.

The roads on the mountain get a lot worse than these highways, and there's a lot less room for . . . error." She put extra weight on the last word. "You can probably make it to town, but I'd advise you to grab a room at the motel there and stay put. You can make the rest of your trip when the storm has passed and the plows have had a chance to clear things up a bit."

"Thanks for the advice," Alex said. "We'll think about it."

She nodded. "Smart thing to do is stay in town. Don't say I didn't warn you." She slapped the bottom of the window frame twice. "I'll let you get on your way. Have a good trip, and above all else, be careful."

"Thanks, Officer," they all said, not quite in unison. Alex rolled the window back up and started driving down the shoulder until he'd gotten up to speed. Then he merged back on to the highway, and the police car disappeared in the snow behind them.

CHAPTER
4

They'd been silent for nearly a half hour. Even Leo was quietly looking out his window at the pure white landscape flying by.

The storm had gotten worse. Much worse. The wind had picked up and kept blowing snow across the road. There were moments where CJ was sure they were going to drive straight into a ditch because there was no way Alex could see the road. He had decreased the speed of the van, but CJ was worried they were still going too fast. At its best, visibility was down to about thirty feet, and she kept picturing red brake lights suddenly appearing in front of them and the van being unable to stop in time.

"Maybe we should slow down a little more," she suggested.

She half expected Alex to protest. He'd seemed pretty wound up since the argument. Maybe he was just stressed because of the drive, but she thought something else might be bothering him. Either way, the van's speed decreased from thirty-five to twenty-five, and CJ felt better.

Leo pulled out his phone and typed the cabin's address into the GPS app. "We're about fifty miles out," he said. "Normally, I think we'd be able to see the mountain from here, but . . ." He gestured out the window.

"At this rate," CJ said dryly, "we'll get there in two hours." She regretted saying it the moment it came out of her mouth. She'd just been thinking out loud, but all she'd done was remind Alex that he had two hours of this miserable drive left. Not only that, but according to the timeline they'd planned, they should already be sitting on a lift on their way up the mountain.

They all fell silent again, and CJ considered

the possibility of turning around. It would be a waste—a waste of time, effort, and the money they'd paid for the lift passes, but maybe it was the right thing to do. The worst part of the storm was supposed to pass right over Colorado, so if they turned around, the driving would remain dangerous for a while, but it would only get better.

No, CJ thought. *Everything will be fine. There's no reason to call off an entire trip just because of a little discomfort. Once we're there, we'll be happy we stuck with it.* She decided the worst-case scenario would be that they stayed in the motel in town like the police officer had suggested. They could head up to the cabin the next morning and only lose a day of hitting the slopes. That wasn't so bad.

"Anybody want to play another game?" Leo asked. "Get our minds off the storm?"

"I'd rather not," Katrina said flatly.

"Yeah," CJ said. "We should let Alex focus on driving."

Leo nodded. "Fair enough."

A few more minutes of silence went by. CJ

watched the storm get worse and worse. Either the snow was falling harder or the wind was blowing more. It was hard to tell which, but it was definitely becoming a disaster out there. Alex had slowed to twenty miles per hour, and he was still passing a few cars. One or two had even pulled over to the side of the road, their taillights glowing as the van passed.

CJ wondered what their plan was. *Are they going to wait out the entire storm on the shoulder? By the time it's over, their cars will be completely buried.* As quickly as the cars appeared in the storm, they vanished from her sight.

Watching conditions worsen was only making CJ more nervous. She didn't want to distract Alex, but she figured they could all use something to get their minds off the storm. She leaned forward between Leo and Alex and changed the station on the radio. This one played an old blues song, and she only had time to hear a wailing lyric about a girl who'd done the singer wrong before she turned the knob again. The next station was playing pop music, and she sat back in her seat.

The distraction of music helped a bit, but it was impossible for them to forget about the storm. It was literally all they could look at unless they chose to stare at the floor of the van.

The music only played for a couple minutes before it cut out. Three loud beeps played through the radio, followed by a voice. "This is an urgent message from the Colorado Department of Transportation," the voice said. "A travel advisory has been issued for all counties due to severe weather conditions. Citizens are advised against travel of any kind until ten a.m. tomorrow morning. Again, a travel advisory has been issued . . ." Leo turned off the radio as the message repeated itself.

"We should turn back," Katrina said.

"We're not turning back," Alex said. "I can get us there."

"I'm with Alex on this one," Leo said. "It's the whole state. If we turn back, we've still got a good chunk of Colorado to drive through. We'd just be on the road even longer. The safest thing to do now is just to push through."

"I agree," CJ said. "But I don't think we should go all the way to the cabin. If the roads are this bad on the highway, they're going to be a lot worse on the mountain. We should stop at that motel. I'll call my parents and ask if I can use the credit card they gave me. How far from town are we?"

Leo checked his phone. He was quiet for a moment, then said, " "Umm, I don't know."

"What does the map say?" Katrina asked.

"Well," Leo said. "If this is to be believed, we're currently right around *connection lost* and maybe a few minutes from *searching for service*." He held the phone behind him for them to see. Sure enough, the phone screen showed a pixelated map that had frozen before it could fully load. A small wheel turned over and over as the phone struggled to catch a signal.

CJ and Katrina each pulled out their own phones. The little triangle that indicated the strength of her signal was completely empty. "I guess I'm not calling my parents," CJ said.

"I've got nothing," Katrina said, tapping at her screen.

"It's got to be the storm," Leo said as he slid his phone back into his pocket.

"It doesn't matter," Alex said. "I told you all I can get us there."

CJ glanced over Alex's shoulder and looked at the gas gauge. They had a little less than a quarter of a tank left. "When we get to town, we'll need gas anyway. Stop at the first gas station you see, and we'll just ask where the motel is."

"I thought you needed to get your parents' permission to use that card," Katrina said.

"They said it's for emergencies," CJ replied. "I think this qualifies. Let's use it, and I'll explain later. The motel's landline phones probably work."

"Sounds like a plan," Leo said.

CJ felt a weight lift off her shoulders. She was nervous enough about being out on the highways during this storm—she didn't even want to think about what driving up those narrow mountain roads would be like. She remembered them from last year. Even in good conditions, they could be terrifying in places. There were steep drop-offs and outright cliffs. One wrong move or an unfortunate slip could send them all falling to their deaths. Waiting out the storm in the comfort of the motel was easily the better option.

Within twenty minutes, they saw the glow of a gas station's tall sign just off the highway. Alex carefully steered the car down the exit ramp and headed toward the station. He pulled the van up to the first pump, and they all got out.

The storm was somehow worse than CJ had thought. From inside the car, everything had looked so evenly white that it had been difficult to tell how much snow had actually fallen, but when CJ stepped outside, the snow nearly reached her knee. Some of it fell into her boots, immediately soaking her socks. The wind had gotten colder and stronger than when they'd spoken to the police officer. It tore at CJ's skin like a knife, and she buried her face in her coat to protect herself from it.

While Alex filled the tank, the others went inside the station, startling the one employee, who obviously wasn't expecting anyone to arrive in the awful weather.

"Excuse me," CJ said to him. "Is there a motel nearby?"

He blinked at her for a second but then replied, "Yeah, it's just down the road." He gave them directions.

They bought a few snacks and drinks, and Leo grabbed a board game from one of the shelves. "Got to do something while we wait out the storm, right?" he said when CJ saw he was actually going to buy it.

They piled back in the van just as Alex finished refilling the gas tank. CJ told him where to find the motel, but he didn't respond, just started up the van and pulled out of the gas station.

CJ breathed a sigh of relief. The worst parts of this journey seemed to be over. They'd wait out the storm, and tomorrow, once the plows had cleared the road, they could drive the rest of the way and get on with the fun . . . assuming Alex and Katrina could control themselves.

Up ahead, CJ could just make out the road where they were supposed to make a left through the snow. But then, much to her surprise, the van kept going.

"Whoa, whoa, whoa," Leo said. "It's a left—a left!"

Alex turned to the right. He didn't say anything, didn't slow down, didn't even acknowledge what was happening. As they passed under a green highway sign, CJ realized he was going to keep driving up the mountain.

"I think you missed the turn there, buddy," Leo said. His tone was caught somewhere between jokey and irritated. "You got a plan . . . or something?"

"Turn around, Alex!" Katrina shouted from the back seat.

Alex just kept driving.

"Alex, what are you doing?" CJ asked, trying to keep her voice calm.

"I can make it," he replied quietly. "I'll get us there."

CJ turned to Leo and gave him her 'help me out here' face.

"No one's saying you can't make it,"

Leo said. "It's more about not *having* to make it. We can stay in the motel, and once the storm's cleared up, the drive will be easy. This," he gestured out the windshield, "is the worst. Do you really *want* to go to the cabin right now . . . in this?"

"I'll be fine," he said as quietly as before.

"We agreed to go to the motel!" Katrina shouted. "Turn around!"

"No!" Alex shouted suddenly. "How many times do I have to tell you I can get us there?"

"Alex." CJ put a hand on his shoulder and hoped that it would calm him down. "It's okay. This drive has got to be incredibly stressful, and we've been backseat driving the whole time. We're not doubting your ability to get us up the mountain, but like Leo said, tomorrow the drive will be super easy. Just turn around, and we can all relax in the motel until things have cleared up. It's just a better way to go about doing this."

"I can get us to the cabin," Alex replied firmly. "If you want to make it easier on me, stop telling me what to do and let me get us there."

Katrina leaned forward, clearly about to shout at Alex to turn around again, but CJ put a hand on her shoulder. Katrina looked at her, and CJ shook her head. Going up the mountain in these conditions was a terrible idea, but having a shouting match at the same time was a recipe for disaster. Katrina gritted her teeth and sat back in her seat.

"Okay, Alex," CJ said. "Just promise you'll be careful, okay?"

"I'll be careful," Alex said, a lot calmer now.

"Again," Leo said carefully, "not questioning your ability, but do you actually know where you're going without the GPS?"

"Katrina and I have been to the cabin a bunch of times," Alex said flatly. "I know how to get there, and we should be able to see the mailbox from the road even in this blizzard." While the others went quiet, CJ tried to convince herself that they'd make it to the cabin in one piece. Alex said he'd be careful, and he was doing exactly that. His speed was slow and reasonable. He kept his eyes on the road, and his attention didn't seem to be wavering from the drive. If anything, he was more focused than ever.

Still, she could picture the drop-offs and cliffs from the drive last year. CJ wasn't afraid of heights. In fact, she loved heights. Part of what she loved most about snowboarding was looking down from the top of the hill. What scared her was falling. If Alex made even one wrong move on the mountain roads, that's what would happen—a free fall.

CJ tried to think of the positives. There was ice on the road, but there weren't many cars driving. That meant they wouldn't have to worry about passing other vehicles on the road. The roads were extremely narrow, and last year, they'd had to slow down to a crawl a few times just to make sure they didn't side-swipe another car going the opposite direction.

Before long, the van started up an incline. CJ couldn't even see the mountain through the blizzard.

The van started spinning out, moving at only a few miles per hour even though CJ could hear Alex giving it more gas. It seemed like they might get stuck right there at the bottom of the mountain, but after a moment, the van lurched forward and began moving at its normal pace.

CJ leaned back in her seat and closed her eyes. Watching out the window was just stressing her out. Maybe keeping her eyes shut would help.

She nearly fell asleep after a half hour, but her eyes shot open when she had an edge-of-sleep vision of the van tumbling down the side of a cliff.

When CJ looked around, at first she questioned whether or not they were truly headed up the mountain. Everything looked mostly the same as when they were on the relatively flat highway. She stared out the window trying to see the road, a signpost—anything that would help her get her bearings.

The wind whipped up, and for one terrible moment, CJ clearly saw the one thing she hoped she wouldn't—a cliff. A few feet away, across one narrow lane of traffic, the land dropped off dramatically into a valley filled with trees and boulders.

She jerked away from the window when she realized what she was looking at. More snow fell, and the valley vanished in the haze of the snow. She looked out Katrina's window. Alex was hugging the right side of the road as best he could. The only thing between the van and the steep mountain wall on the right was a snowbank, a giant drift created by all the blowing snow.

"You okay?" Katrina asked her. Leo turned in his seat to see what was going on.

"Yeah," CJ replied. "I almost fell asleep, and I was just startled when I looked out the window."

"These roads get really high really quickly," Leo said. CJ didn't need that explained to her, and she was a little annoyed Leo had bothered to say anything. She remembered the roads from last year just as well as he did.

"How much farther do we have to go?" she asked, desperately trying to avoid looking to the left.

"Not far," Alex said from the driver's seat. "But it's slow going."

CJ couldn't help but notice that Alex hadn't even bothered to guess at how long the drive would actually take, and she wondered if he knew.

The road turned one way, then the other. Even in good weather, she'd hated this part last year. The path up the mountain to the cabin was rarely straight. It swerved all over the place, doubled back on itself, narrowed and got wider in places, all at a constant upward angle.

Last year, CJ had distracted herself with games and conversation with her friends. And she hadn't worried as much about the idea of the van slipping off the road, since she'd been able to see the drop-offs.

Suddenly, something seemed wrong. Alex cranked the wheel from left to right. There was a sort of grinding noise coming from below the van, but without being able to make out anything clearly through the snow, CJ had no idea what the problem was. As Alex jerked on the wheel, the other passengers were pulled back and forth. CJ's stomach churned as she got swept up in the movement.

The van came to a very sudden halt. CJ got her hands up just in time to avoid smacking her head on Alex's seat in front of her.

"What happened?" Leo asked.

"Nothing," Alex said firmly. "We just spun out a little and hit the snowbank."

"Are we stuck?" Katrina asked loudly. CJ couldn't tell if she was angry or worried.

"No," Alex snapped. "We're not stuck. I just need to maneuver us out."

It looked like Katrina was about to yell at Alex again, but CJ cut her off before she could. "Okay, just be careful about it."

Alex muttered something under his breath and shifted the van into reverse. Looking over his shoulder, he gave it a little gas. The engine revved, but it didn't move. He muttered again, turned the wheel and tried a little more gas.

"You're going to drive us off the road!" Katrina said.

"No, I'm not!"

Alex tried spinning the wheel the other way. More gas, but once again, nothing happened. He tried three more times before he shifted it into park.

"I think we're stuck, dude," Leo said.

"Great," Katrina said sarcastically. "That's perfect, Alex."

"It's not like I was trying to—"

"Let's just get out and take a look," CJ said, pulling on her jacket, hat, and gloves. "It's probably an easy fix." She opened the door, and the wind cut off anything anyone was about to say.

As bad as the wind had been at the gas station, it was much worse this far up the mountain. It was stronger and colder than CJ thought possible. Her outer layers made little to no difference in the brutal conditions. The snow was almost to her knees, going up past her winter boots. She looked behind her and could see there was a very obvious path where the van had come from, spinout and all.

CJ was amazed they had made it as far as they had. Getting the van out of the snowbank was going to be next to impossible.

"We're never going to get out of this!" Katrina shouted over the wind.

"Maybe with some digging," Leo said. "We can—"

"I can get us out," Alex cut him off. "Just give me a little more time, and—"

"You're not going to get us out, Alex!" Katrina said. "You're the one that got us *in* this mess in the first place! All you had to do was stop at the motel!"

There was no stopping this latest explosion. CJ was tired of playing the peacemaker. This time she just folded her arms and watched her two friends.

"Everything's always *my* fault, isn't it?" raged Alex. "Maybe if we hadn't lost time on the side of the highway because you were screaming in my ear, we would have beaten the storm!"

"I wouldn't have been shouting in your ear if you weren't being such a jerk about college!"

"We had agreed to go to UCLA!"

"*You* decided to go to UCLA and that I would go there too. I never agreed, and if this is how you're going to act for the next four years, I'm not even going to think about going there!"

"Well, right now, I don't *want* you to come with me anyway!" Alex shouted.

"Perfect!" Katrina fired back. "And while we're at it, let's just break up!"

"Fine!" Alex whipped around and got back into the van.

CHAPTER
6

As Alex slammed the door shut behind him, Katrina shuffled her way through the snow, across the street and down the road. She stared into the valley with her arms crossed against her chest.

Leo and CJ watched her from where they were still standing in the road. CJ didn't know what to do now. "This trip is going great," Leo said. "Maybe we should all just take a gap year and live together in the wilderness now that we're out here."

"Jokes? Really, Leo?"

He gave her a goofy grin. "Sometimes that's all I've got."

CJ couldn't help herself from smiling at him. "You talk to Alex. I'll talk to Katrina."

"You sure?" he replied. "Whoever talks to Alex gets to sit in the warm van."

She shrugged. Even though her fingers and face were freezing, she shuffled over to where Katrina was standing.

When she got close enough, she could see that Katrina had been crying. One of her tears was frozen just under her eye. Her lashes were covered in ice, and they seemed to be sticking together every time she blinked.

"Are you okay?" CJ asked.

Katrina tried to wipe some of the ice out of her eyes. "Yeah, I'm just mad. We shouldn't have taken this trip."

You *shouldn't have taken this trip*, CJ thought. *It could have been fun, but you two have made a real mess of things.* She felt bad for thinking it. Maybe it was selfish, but it was true.

"It's okay," she said. "We're all a little on edge because of the drive and the storm. This will all blow over once we're—"

"No, it won't," Katrina interrupted. "He's

been a jerk for months. Going to a cabin isn't going to make a difference." She wiped another frozen tear from her cheek.

CJ looked back at the van. She couldn't see either Alex or Leo because the snow was coming down so quickly that even in the short time the van had been still, it had covered the windows completely. It was a deadly serious reminder that even with what had just happened, they needed to get the van out of the snowbank and get out of there before they were trapped beyond the point of escape.

"Well," CJ said. "We're almost to the cabin already. Turning back now would be . . ." She looked down the road in the direction the van had come from. The tire tracks were still there, but the snow was already rapidly filling them. "It would be worse than continuing. Like it or not, we're going on this trip."

Katrina looked back at the van, but CJ couldn't read her expression.

"Think of it this way," she continued. "You're going on a ski trip with your friends, and Alex . . . Alex just happens to be there."

Katrina turned back to her and sighed, clearly unconvinced.

"Okay," CJ said. "Then think of it *this* way: you don't really have a choice, so try to not to make it harder than it needs to be."

"Fine. Let's just get this over with." She trudged her way toward the van, and CJ followed behind her.

Alex and Leo got out just as the other two were approaching. The trunk popped open, and Alex went over to it and dug around beneath their luggage and equipment. He pulled out a shovel and a windshield scraper.

Standing around the van, CJ wasn't sure they'd be able to get the vehicle out of the snowbank. The front was completely buried under white powder, and the path behind it was just getting thicker with the stuff.

"The longer we wait," Leo said, "the harder this is going to be. We should get started." He took the tools from Alex and handed CJ the scraper, keeping the shovel himself. "I'll dig out the snow. CJ, use this to break up the ice. Maybe the wheels will get a little traction that way."

"I'll keep trying to give it a little gas, see if I can get it loose," said Alex. He started heading toward the driver's door when Katrina scoffed. He turned to her and glared. "What?"

"So, you get to sit in the warm van while the rest of us fix your mistake? *You* should dig us out."

"Someone has to drive the van. Do you want to do it?" Alex asked angrily.

"I'm not helping to clean up your mess."

"So, you'd rather be stuck on a mountain than lift a finger to—"

"Stop!" CJ said, holding up a hand. "Both of you just . . . stop. It's going to take all of us to get this thing loose. Everyone helps. Katrina, if you don't want to shovel, drive the van. Alex, help us shovel."

"With what?" he snapped.

"Your hands, unless you've got a better idea."

Alex blinked at her as Katrina got in the driver's seat.

"Look, we don't have time for more drama," CJ said to him. "Let's do this."

They got to work digging out the back

tires. Once Leo and Alex got the majority of snow out from behind the tires, CJ chipped away at the ice and packed snow. It was bitter cold, and the work was hard. Snow kept making its way down the back of her coat, up her sleeves, and into her boots. And as cold as that was, with all the digging, she was beginning to sweat beneath all her layers.

They worked and worked, but the falling snow was undoing a lot of what they accomplished, filling in what they dug out. Sometimes, CJ thought they weren't making any progress at all, but they all kept going until they thought they'd cleared enough.

"Okay," Leo shouted to Katrina over the howl of the wind. "Try it now."

Katrina gave it some gas, but the van didn't budge.

"Try it again," Leo said. "But give it a little more this time."

Katrina tried again. All three of the others put their hands on the hood and pushed. This time, the van rocked backward slightly but didn't budge.

Alex threw his hands in the air in frustration. "Give it more than that! See? I should be the one driving!"

"I'm being careful, Alex!" Katrina shouted.

"You're being too careful! It needs more gas to get out!"

"If I give it too much, it'll spin out again!"

"Then don't give it too much!" Alex shouted. "Give it the right amount!"

"Thanks, Alex," Katrina snapped. "That's really helpful advice."

"Not to rush you," CJ said as calmly as she could, "but if we don't get this thing unstuck soon, it's going to be here a long time and so are we."

"See?" Alex shouted. "CJ agrees with me!"

"That's not what I—" CJ started.

"Give it more gas!" Alex shouted before she had a chance to finish.

CJ could see Katrina getting angrier and angrier. She was glaring at Alex, practically shooting daggers from her eyes.

"What are you waiting for?" he shouted.

"You want me to give it more gas?" Katrina

spat as she turned back to the steering wheel. "Fine! Tell me if this is enough!"

The engine roared to life. Katrina must have floored it. CJ saw the tires spinning, and then suddenly they caught. The van jerked backward.

For a split second, CJ was thrilled. The van had come free and they could get on with the trip, maybe even patch things up once they were at the cabin . . . but her excitement turned to terror when the van didn't stop going backward. It shot across the road and over the drop-off with Katrina still inside.

CHAPTER
7

The van didn't fall far. It only dropped about fifteen feet, where it smashed against a tree. It spun when it dropped, so it landed on its right side.

CJ, Leo, and Alex hovered at the edge of the drop-off, surveying the damage. The rear passenger door was caved in where it had hit the tree. It was pure luck that Katrina was still alive. If the tree had been just five feet to the left or right, the van would have rolled all the way down into the valley, taking Katrina with it.

"Katrina!" Alex shouted, his eyes wide.

They could see her shifting in the driver's seat, trying to get her bearings. Fortunately, she was wearing her seatbelt. "Don't move!" CJ shouted. "We're coming!" The van didn't look like it was in a stable position. The tree it was stuck against was thick, but if the vehicle was even a little off-center, the slightest movement could cause it to shift and fall.

Leo had his hands on his head as if he were trying to pull his hair out. "What do we do?"

"We get her out of there!" CJ shouted. Even as she said it, she saw it was going to be easier said than done.

The drop-off was steep, much too steep for any one of them to walk down, grab Katrina, and walk back up again, especially if Katrina was injured.

Katrina rolled the window down, and only then did CJ realize the van was still running, even while smashed up against a tree.

"Help!" she yelled.

"Are you hurt?" CJ yelled back.

Katrina looked around for a second. "No . . . no, I don't think so."

"I'll get her," Leo said.

"No, hold on!" CJ said. "Even if you make it to her, you'd have no way of getting back up here."

"Well, how do we get her then?"

CJ had never seen Leo panic like this. He was always the calm one, cracking jokes even when tensions were running high. Now, she could see pure fear in his eyes.

"I've got an idea," Alex said. He grabbed a small tree by the edge of the drop-off and shook it, testing its strength. "I'll hold on to this tree and lower Leo down. You can grab onto one of his hands, he can lower you down, and maybe you can reach Katrina."

CJ didn't like the sound of the plan. It was risky, and it meant she would be dangling down the steep slope. One mistake, and she'd be falling. *But*, she realized as she gritted her teeth, *there aren't really any other options.* "Okay," she said.

"Stay there and stay still," Alex called to Katrina. "We're coming to get you!"

He gripped the tree. He adjusted his hold on it a few times and tested the strength of the trunk once more. Alex grabbed Leo's hand, and CJ grabbed Leo's.

Slowly but surely, they started sliding their way down the drop-off.

"You got us?" Leo asked when Alex was fully stretched out, lowering the two of them as far as he could.

"Yeah," he said, although he sounded strained. "I've got you."

Leo lowered CJ down as far as he could. She was closer to the van than she thought she'd be, easily within reach of Katrina. The thought of all their stuff—their money, their IDs, their cell phone chargers, their extra clothes—in the van's trunk flashed through her mind. Assuming they could get Katrina to safety, they should probably also try to recover their gear.

"You ready?" CJ said. She was close enough that she didn't have to shout over the wind.

Katrina nodded and unclipped her seatbelt.

"Okay, pop the trunk and cut the engine, and then come on out," CJ said. If they left the engine running, the van might be completely out of gas by the time they could call a tow service to retrieve it. CJ felt strangely calm as these thoughts came to her, as if part of her brain had switched off her fear and started logically thinking ahead.

Katrina did as she was told. Once she got the door open, she shifted in the seat until her foot was against the center console. She pushed up, grabbed CJ's hand, and hoisted herself out of the van.

CJ pulled her up with all of her might. Her feet dug into the snow for traction, and her arm strained as Katrina leaned all her weight into CJ.

"Okay," CJ shouted. "Help us up!"

She heard both Leo and Alex grunt and strain. Finally, with a lot of pulling and getting as much traction as they could against the hill, they made it back to the road, safe and sound . . . *At least for the time being*, CJ thought.

They all looked down at the van. It hadn't moved an inch, even with Katrina shifting inside it.

CJ turned to Alex and Leo. "How many more times do you think you can do that?"

Within a half hour, they had gotten their

stuff out of the back of the van using the same method they had used to rescue Katrina. One suitcase, pair of skis, and snowboard at a time, they retrieved everything they'd brought with them.

Once it was all done, CJ felt a swell of pride. Not only had she confronted her fear of falling, she had done it multiple times by choice.

"Which way do we go?" Leo asked the group.

They were all a little out of breath. They'd been successful in getting their stuff back, but lowering themselves and coming back up over and over again had been tiring.

Leo turned to Katrina. "How far are we from the cabin?"

She looked around for a second. "I can't really tell in this storm."

"If you had to guess," Leo urged. "Are we closer to the cabin or town?"

After thinking for a second, she replied, "The cabin . . . I think."

"You think?" Alex said harshly. "You think or you know?"

"I *think*, Alex."

"I *would* have made it the rest of the way if *you* hadn't driven it off a cliff." Alex was getting louder.

"Give it more gas!" Katrina shouted at him, mimicking his voice. "Does that sound familiar?"

"I didn't mean give it so much that you shoot over the edge, you—"

"Shut up!" CJ screamed. "Both of you, shut up! If you two had gotten over your stupid argument, *none* of us would be in this situation. I don't care *whose* fault it is! In case you haven't noticed, we've got much bigger problems right now. We're stuck on a mountain, and unless you want to freeze to death up here, we need to make decisions quickly."

Alex and Katrina both looked down at their boots.

"Once we're safe and warm, you two can blame each other, scream at each other, or tear each other's throats out for all I care," she continued. "Until then, shut up!"

There was a beat of silence. Alex and

Katrina continued staring at the ground, and Leo gave her an impressed look.

"Katrina thinks we're closer to the cabin, so we go up the mountain," CJ said firmly. "Grab your stuff. Put on as many layers as you can. She unzipped her suitcase. "And then we need to move."

They all quickly put on their heavy-duty snowboarding or ski boots and snow pants. They layered sweaters and sweatshirts underneath their jackets and stuffed their hands into their thick gloves.

Each of them had a strap attached to their snowboards or skis to make them easier to carry. They hooked the gear over their backs, leaving their hands free so they could drag their wheeled suitcases behind them. The trek wouldn't be easy, but at least they were taking action.

The four of them, still unsure of how far from the cabin they truly were, began the trek up the mountain road.

CHAPTER
8

CJ couldn't stop thinking about how many TV shows she'd watched in which one of the characters said, "At least things can't get any worse." That meant things were about to get worse—usually a lot worse. She felt that way about the blizzard. She'd thought it many times during the drive, and the storm always proved her wrong. She made the fatal mistake of thinking it just before they started walking, and once again, the storm was proving her dreadfully wrong.

The wind sliced at every inch of exposed skin. Every time a blast of cold wind blew into her face, she felt like her breath was caught.

Even swallowing was difficult. Frost had formed around the mouth of her ski mask, which was doing next to nothing in these conditions. Her coat and snow gear were warm but heavy, so her legs quickly began to ache as they trudged through the snow. And dragging their bags with them didn't make the hike any easier.

They'd only been walking for forty-five minutes.

Even if the road had been clear, the walk probably would have been difficult due to the constant incline. While CJ had been proud of her ability to conquer her fear and get their belongings from the trunk, now she almost regretted it. The bags were a burden, maybe an unnecessary one.

"Should we just leave our suitcases?" she asked the group.

Leo, leading the trail, and Alex, just behind him, turned around. "What?" she heard Leo yell through the wind.

She repeated her question. "We can't," Katrina said from behind her. "If we make it to the cabin, we might be there for a while, especially if this storm doesn't let up. We'll need clothes and stuff."

"What?" Leo shouted again, unable to hear anyone over the howling wind. Alex turned back toward him and repeated what CJ had asked.

Leo turned back to her and shouted, "We'll want the spare clothes and stuff when we get to the cabin."

She rolled her eyes. "I got that. Okay, we'll keep the suitcases." Still, she fished her wallet out of her suitcase and zipped it up in her coat pocket with her currently useless phone. That way if she had to abandon the suitcase later, she'd still have her money and ID with her.

They continued on.

The longer they walked, the slower their progress became. The snow covered most of their legs, and moving through it was like trying to walk through a pool filled with packing peanuts.

CJ forced herself to put one foot in front of

the other as they made their way up the road. With each turn they rounded, she hoped the cabin's mailbox would be right in front of them, but it never was. Besides the occasional tree, all she could see in any direction was pure white.

She began to doubt their ability to make it there at all. If the storm continued like this, it would only be an hour, maybe two, before they were all too tired to keep moving. They would be stuck with no shelter, no warmth, and no hope. She started considering the possibility that she, Leo, Katrina, and Alex would die on this mountain.

The wind was arguably worse than the snow. When it whipped up into a strong gust, the four were forced to hunker down as much as they could because it was simply unbearable.

Leo stopped. Alex, looking at the ground to keep the wind out of his face, bumped right into him. They leaned their heads together so they could hear one another talk. CJ and Katrina, who were trailing behind them, waded through the snow to join them.

The four of them pressed together in a tight circle for warmth.

Leo looked at CJ and said, "Alex wants to keep going, but I don't know."

"We can't be far," Alex said.

"Do you know for sure?" CJ asked.

She looked at Katrina as Alex shook his head. "It could be around the next corner or a mile farther," Katrina said. "Without being able to see the landmarks, I can't say for certain."

"Do we have a choice anymore?" Alex asked. "Going back down will be just as slow and definitely farther than the cabin."

"I don't know how much more of this I can take," Leo said.

"Alex is right, though," CJ said. "Even if we had cell reception, I don't think anyone could get to us right now."

"Maybe we should camp out somewhere and try to stick it out," Leo suggested.

"There's no way we'd survive this, Leo!" CJ said. "If we stay out here much longer, we could get really sick—or worse."

"Well, maybe we go back to the van! At least we'd be a little warmer in there."

"It was teetering on a cliff!" Katrina said.

"Teetering, not falling," he pointed out.

"And you're assuming we'd be able to find it again," Katrina continued as if Leo hadn't said anything. "At the rate the snow's coming down, it's got to be buried already, and that's not even counting the time it would take us to get back there."

The wind picked up, and the four of them closed in together even more to form a little pod. When they were huddled up like this, it wasn't so bad. The wind whipped at their backs, but it couldn't reach their faces or their hands tucked into their chests.

Before they could continue their debate, CJ heard a rumbling sound. *Thunder,* she thought. It started as a dull roar, but it got stronger and stronger until she could actually feel it shaking the ground beneath her. *I didn't know blizzards could produce thunder.*

Alex popped his head up from the huddle and seemed to be looking around. Suddenly, he started pushing all three of them. "Run!" he shouted.

CJ and the others practically tripped over themselves as Alex shoved them forward. He grabbed Katrina and Leo's arms in each hand and started dragging them behind him. Leo reached to link hands with CJ as she trailed behind.

CJ didn't know what they were running from until the thunder grew louder behind them, and something clicked into place in her mind.

Avalanche!

CHAPTER 9

The wall of snow dropped down the mountain from above them, knocking them all off their feet and burying them in an instant.

CJ felt herself getting tossed and turned. She lost any sense of direction. The concept of *up* became meaningless as the snow jostled her around. Snow poured down the neck of her coat, completely filled her boots, and even got in her tightly cinched gloves.

When she stopped moving, everything was dark and cold. Snow pressed against her face. She tried to move her right arm, but it wouldn't budge. The left was stuck in place as well. Her suitcase was gone. It had flown out of her hand the moment the avalanche hit her. The snowboard, it seemed, was still strapped to her back.

She started breathing heavily, her body going into panic mode. *I'm going to die right here, stuck in place like a dinosaur trapped in a tar pit*, she thought.

She tried to calm herself down. *Breathe. Just breathe for a couple minutes.* Each breath she took was cold, and some of what she inhaled was snow. *Start with your fingers.*

She wiggled her fingers and found that they could move. It wasn't much, but it was something. She wriggled and spun them around, making a little cavity in the snow. Soon she was able to move her wrist, then her forearm, and she started waving it around as much as she could, loosening the snow that was keeping her in place. She set to work digging a cavity out of the snow surrounding her face.

CJ was breathing so heavily that she kept breathing in snow by accident. Growing frustrated, she spat it out of her mouth. It flew in front of her and dropped to the left. CJ realized that this must be the work of gravity and that up must be to her right.

She swung her arm, loosening more snow to her right until she felt the wind catching on her gloved hand. She'd broken through the snow. She began waving her hand around hoping that Leo, Katrina, or Alex would see it and help her get out. When no one did, she started clearing the snow from above her head. Once her head and most of her torso were free, she was able to pull herself out of the massive snow pile.

She looked around, and fear gripped her harder than the cold. She didn't see anyone. No Leo. No Alex. No Katrina. Everything was pure white, and with all the snow that had just fallen in the avalanche, she couldn't even see the road . . . or wherever the road used to be. It was all one giant snow bank.

She heard a strange rapping sound coming from behind her. As she turned around, she saw a figure in the distance. After a moment she realized the person was frantically digging in the snow. She started moving toward the person, stumbling twice in snow that was up to her chest.

"Leo?" she called out.

The person quickly whipped their head around before returning to continue digging. "Help me!" they shouted back.

It was Alex's voice. As she got closer, CJ realized he was trying to dig someone *out*. CJ made it over to him and started digging where he was. Before long, they uncovered a hat, and Katrina snapped her head around, taking a deep breath as she did so.

"Get me out of here!" she shouted.

Alex and CJ dug as hard as they could. Eventually, Katrina was able to get herself free from the snow.

"Where's Leo?" CJ asked.

"I haven't seen him," Alex said, panting. "I crawled out, and the first thing I saw was Katrina's hand sticking out of the snow."

"Oh my god," CJ breathed, feeling her stomach drop. She tried not to let herself think of the worst.

Katrina started shouting Leo's name.

CJ and Alex did the same.

They called and called, but nothing came back. Leo was nowhere to be seen. As the wind died down, CJ caught sight of the drop-off. It wasn't that far away from them. She took a sharp breath inward. *He fell*, she thought. *The avalanche knocked him over the side.*

She felt her legs go weak and would have fallen to her knees if the deep snow wasn't preventing her from doing so. Alex and Katrina were still calling out, but with each time the call wasn't returned, CJ felt more and more hopeless. He was gone.

Alex gave up first, shuffling his way over to CJ and hugging her. Shortly after, Katrina stopped shouting. She stood in the snow looking toward the drop-off without moving, and CJ figured she had realized what happened. CJ felt tears welling up in her eyes.

"Hey!" It was Leo's voice.

CHAPTER
10

CJ's head snapped around, frantically scanning the area, but she couldn't see Leo.

"Hey!" he shouted again. "Help!"

Katrina seemed to know where the voice was coming from. She pushed her way through the snow, with CJ and Alex coming up behind her.

Somehow, Leo had managed to land on a ledge about six feet down into the drop-off. The ledge had stayed mostly free of snow, but it was so narrow that he was struggling to stay on top of it in the wind. He crouched low, one hand clinging to the rock face beside him and the other gripping the side of the ledge.

"I'm coming!" CJ said, moving to slide down the drop-off.

"Wait." Alex grabbed her shoulder. He tested the strength of a tree at the edge of the drop-off near where they were standing. "We've done this before." He gripped the tree tightly and held his other hand out for CJ to take.

It was harder this time. CJ had to push snow out of the way with her feet and free hand, but gradually she slid her way down to Leo. She dislodged some snow that fell straight onto his face. Leo flinched as it happened, but he kept his grip.

"I've got you," she said, grabbing his wrist and bringing his arm around her waist. Leo stood on shaky legs.

"If this were on TV," he said, "I'll bet the episode would end here."

CJ stared at him.

"You know . . . on a cliff-hanger."

She was too stressed to laugh. "You're the worst. You ready?" He nodded and lifted his other hand up for Alex and Katrina to grab along with CJ's.

"Okay," CJ called up to them, "pull!"

As Katrina and Alex lifted them, CJ and Leo started walking their feet up the rock face to help. CJ's muscles burned and felt like they were about to tear at any moment, but they were slowly coming up. After a couple difficult minutes, they climbed over the edge to solid ground.

Leo groaned and flopped back into the snow, and the rest of them joined him as they caught their breath.

It wasn't until she sat down that CJ noticed Katrina was clutching one bare hand to her chest. A hand that was a deep shade of red. "Katrina," she said. "Your hand . . ."

"I lost a glove," Katrina said quietly.

CJ's breath caught in her throat. If Katrina ended up with frostbite, she could permanently damage her fingers or even lose them entirely.

Alex turned to her worriedly. "Why didn't you say something sooner?"

"We were trying to find Leo!"

"Here," CJ said. She dug through her coat pocket to find a wool mitten. "I have an extra.

It's not as good as your ski gloves, but it's better than nothing."

Katrina happily took the mitten, tucking her fingers and thumb together into the main pocket to keep them as warm as possible.

"I have to say," Leo said then. "This trip has not been my favorite ski trip so far."

Maybe it was the exhaustion, maybe it was how ridiculous every step of this trip had been, but they all cracked up at that.

Then they got up and piled into a big group hug. For a moment, CJ felt happy. But reality quickly set back in. They were still stranded.

"We have to go back down," Katrina said with a sigh.

She was right, but CJ still hated to hear it out loud. It was so discouraging after what they'd been through to get this far.

Her muscles hurt right down to the bones from the strain of everything that had happened. She was cold and wet from snow that had made its way under her layers and melted. While the storm hadn't gotten any worse, it wasn't getting any better either. The wind was still blowing forcefully. Snow continued to pile on top of what had already fallen.

"There's no other choice," Alex confirmed, gesturing to where the avalanche had completely covered the road.

It was now impossible for CJ to tell where the road was even supposed to be. It all looked like a giant hill. They'd been lucky. It looked as if only the edge of the avalanche had truly struck them, and that was the only reason they'd been able to dig themselves out. If they'd been even a little farther up the road nearer the cabin, there would have been several feet of snow over their heads rather than the several inches they'd had to dig their ways out of.

"We'll never make it," CJ mumbled.

"We have to try, even if it seems impossible," Leo said. "I didn't come inches from falling off a cliff just to die in the snow."

Katrina was the first to start walking. "Let's go," she said.

They'd all lost their suitcases when the wall of snow smashed into them, though they still had their ski gear strapped to their backs. Walking was easier without the luggage, and it also helped that they were now headed down a decline rather than up an incline. Unfortunately, the snow had gotten deeper, and moving through it was that much more difficult.

CJ forced herself to push one foot in front of the other. She and Leo led their group with Alex and Katrina not far behind. CJ's fingers and toes had gone from hurting to numb, even with all the layers she was wearing. Her legs ached with the strain of pushing against several feet of snow. Her back hurt from lugging the snowboard around since they'd left the van. She was breathing deeply, like she'd just run a marathon.

"Because we almost died," CJ heard Alex say suddenly. "Doesn't everything seem clearer to you now?"

"It does, actually," Katrina replied. "But this is *not* the time to talk about it."

CJ and Leo turned around. The other couple had stopped in place, right there in the snow.

"When we got hit by that avalanche, all I could think was that I shouldn't have wasted so much time arguing with you," Alex said. "Even if we end up going to different schools, we don't have to break up."

CJ couldn't believe what she was hearing. All she wanted to do was to get off the mountain to some place safe and warm, but apparently that was less important to her two friends.

"We don't *have* to stay together either," Katrina said. "We've been having this fight for *months*. It's not working, Alex."

"But maybe we can—"

"No," she cut him off. "We can't. And even if we could, I don't think I want to. What I do want is to get off this stupid mountain. Can we just focus on getting home? We can talk about this later."

Alex quietly nodded, and the group began moving toward the bottom of the mountain again. Katrina sped up, almost like she was trying to outrun Alex, but he was willfully lagging behind.

That was uncomfortable, CJ thought. *I wish there were some way to get down the mountain faster—a ski lift or a sled or . . . Of course!* she thought. *Why didn't we think of this sooner?*

"Wait," she said. The others turned to her. "I think there *is* an easier way to get down the mountain. We can ride down it."

"I thought we'd already established that no car would be able to come pick us up in this," Leo said.

She shook her head. "Not a car." She lifted the snowboard over her head and undid the strap before placing the board on the snow.

"You've got to be kidding me," Alex said. "This is a blizzard! We can't—"

"Why not?" CJ cut him off. "Is it any less safe than walking at the pace we're going?"

"We could slide off the edge."

"We could freeze to death if we don't make it to town soon," Leo offered, unstrapping his own board. "I vote that we go for it."

Katrina was already grabbing her skis and poles. "Honestly, I think it's safer than what we're doing right now."

Alex looked like he wanted to protest more, but then he sighed and grabbed the gear out of his own bag.

They were all hooked into their gear and ready to go. They stood in a line waiting. None of them seemed to want to be the first to take what would certainly be the most dangerous run of their lives.

It was my idea, CJ thought. *I should go first.* She shifted the board under her feet so it was angled down the road, and she started sliding. "Follow close," she said over her shoulder to her friends.

She didn't look back, but she heard them each sliding along the snow behind her.

She weaved her board in sharp turns to prevent it from going too fast. She didn't want to take any chances by moving too quickly on such unstable snow. Even at what she considered an extremely slow pace for snowboarding, they were still traveling much faster than they would have been on foot.

Within a few minutes, it seemed like the snow was letting up a bit. CJ was able to see farther down the road and anticipate turns. She called directions over her shoulder to her friends following right behind her.

Most of the road looked the same. Everything was white, covered in thick layers of snow. It didn't take long for them to reach a stretch of road that looked somewhat familiar. There was a rock face to their left and a drop-off to their right. Just down the drop-off, there was a tree with a huge snow-covered lump wrapped around its trunk at the bottom. CJ thought she saw the flash of a taillight on the back of the snow pile as they passed, and she realized how short of a distance they'd actually made it since leaving the van.

Not only was this the most dangerous ride CJ had ever been on, it was also easily the longest. It took nearly an hour and a half of winding, slowing down, speeding up, and hugging the cliff face to avoid the drop-off before the ground began to level off. Only then did CJ realize they were at the bottom of the mountain.

They hadn't seen a single car or plow. If they'd continued walking up the mountain, there really would have been no one to save them.

The ground completely leveled off, and they were no longer able to ride their gear. But in the distance, CJ could see the lights of town. She breathed a huge sigh of relief. They could walk the rest of the way.

They did so in silence, all of them far too tired to even express how relieved they were. CJ didn't know what time it was, but she was sure it was late. Even with the snow coming down on them, the sky seemed dark. When they finally made it to the motel, a bleary-eyed man thumbing through a magazine was obviously surprised to see them. CJ dug her wallet out of her coat and handed him her emergency credit card.

"We need a room."

"That storm's pretty rough for hitting the slopes," the man said, eyeing the gear in their hands.

"Yeah," CJ said. "It is."

CHAPTER
11

CJ grabbed the books she needed for first period and tossed the rest of her stuff in her locker. As she closed the door, she actually felt relieved to be at school. It meant the absolute worst vacation of her life was behind her.

It was also the first day since getting home that CJ was actually feeling better. They'd managed to call their families from the phone in the motel room, and Katrina's dad had hopped into his SUV to come pick them up. By the time he'd gotten to them the next morning, they all had severe colds, and Katrina had developed frostbite in two of her fingers. They spent the majority of the trip home coughing, sneezing, sniffling, and asking Katrina's dad to stop for cold medicine.

CJ's cold had turned into the flu, so she'd spent the rest of winter break in bed. She had heard from Leo regularly, but there was no word from Alex or Katrina.

"May I carry your books for you, Madame?" Leo asked in a terrible British accent as he bowed.

CJ snorted. "I'm good. Thanks though." She didn't feel like joking around when she was still worried about their friends. "Have you heard from Katrina or Alex?"

Leo shrugged. "No, but I assume they worked stuff out, right?"

"Maybe," she said. "Nothing like crashing a car, getting stranded on a mountain and hit by an avalanche, and nearly freezing to death to make your relationship problems seem small."

CJ certainly felt that way about her own college worries. Though she still hadn't heard back from any schools she'd applied to, she knew there was plenty of time for acceptance letters to roll in. And no matter what happened, at least she wasn't buried under six feet of snow in the middle of the wilderness.

"Well, knowing the two of them, I'm sure we'll get an update eventually."

CJ spotted Katrina walking down the hall toward them. "Or we can just ask right now. Hey!" she called, waving.

Katrina came over to them. "How are you guys feeling?"

"Better," CJ said.

"I'm no longer constantly dripping with sweat, so that's good," Leo replied. "How are you?"

Katrina held her hand up, revealing two of her fingers held together in bandages. "It still stings, and the doctors said it'll be another week or so before they stop hurting. Other than that, I'm fine."

"How's Alex?" Leo asked.

"He's good," Katrina said vaguely. "I think he was planning on coming in today, but I haven't heard from him in a couple days."

"Oh, so you *have* been talking . . ."

She rolled her eyes. "Subtle, Leo. But really, the last thing we talked about was that stupid van. I guess after the plows managed to clear the roads on the mountain, his parents were able to pick up the van. Not that they'll be able to use it for a while."

They nodded.

"Seriously, though," CJ said. "What happened?"

Katrina shrugged. "We talked a lot after we both started feeling better. I told Alex I'm going to go to NYU and that he should go to UCLA. It's where he really wants to go, and I want him to go there too."

There was a brief pause.

"And are you two . . ." Leo trailed off.

"We're through. We figured if even the *idea* of doing the long-distance thing put that much of a strain on our relationship, we probably shouldn't be in one. But," she added, "we're not mad at each other anymore. We'll always be friends—long-distance friends—and that's a lot easier."

"Oh," CJ said. "I'm sorry."

Katrina waved it away. "There's nothing to be sorry for. It wasn't working. We both knew that. Now, we're happy and moving on." She glanced at a clock on the hallway wall. "American Lit is on the other side of the building, so I've got to go, but I'll catch you two at lunch?"

"Yeah," CJ said. "See you then."

Katrina walked off.

"Huh," Leo said. "Well, that's probably for the best."

"Yeah. I'm glad they're done arguing about it and we can *all* move on."

He turned to her with a teasing grin. "So, same trip next year?"

CJ's eyes narrowed, but she smiled. "Let's go to the beach next year—*without* another couple."

ABOUT THE AUTHOR

R.T. Martin lives in St. Paul, Minnesota. When he is not drinking coffee or writing, he is busy thinking about drinking coffee and writing.

ROAD
TRIP

HEAT WAVE

OFF COURSE

SPINNING OUT

STRANDED

DAY OF DISASTER

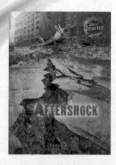

Would you survive?

ATTACK ON EARTH

WHEN ALIENS INVADE, ALL YOU CAN DO IS SURVIVE.

DESERTED

THE FALLOUT

THE FIELD TRIP

GETTING HOME

LOCKDOWN

TAKE SHELTER

CHECK OUT ALL THE TITLES IN THE

ATTACK ON EARTH SERIES

MASON FALLS MYSTERIES

EVEN AN ORDINARY TOWN HAS ITS SECRETS.